LEARN TO

DETECTIVE DAN

and the

Gooey Gumdrop Mystery

written and illustrated by

Timothy Roland

ZondervanPublishingHouse
Grand Rapids, Michigan
A Division of HarperCollinsPublishers

Detective Dan and the Gooey Gumdrop Mystery
Copyright © 1993 by Timothy Roland

Requests for information should be addressed to:
Zondervan Publishing House
Grand Rapids, Michigan 49530

Library of Congress Cataloging-in-Publication Data

Roland, Timothy.
    Detective Dan and the gooey gumdrop mystery / Timothy Roland.
      p. cm.
    Summary: Detective Dan solves the case of the lost treasure map
and shares a Bible verse about sharing with his friend Bernard.
    ISBN 0-310-38111-8 (pbk.)
    [1. Mystery and detective stories. 2. Lost and found possessions
—Fiction. 3. Sharing—Fiction. 4. Christian life—Fiction.]
    I. Title.
PZ7.R6433De   1993
[E]–dc20   93-3497
                                                                CIP
                                                                AC

Edited by Dave Lambert and Leslie Kimmelman
Interior and cover design by Steven M. Scott
Illustrations by Timothy Roland

Printed in the United States of America

93 94 95 96 97 98 / CH / 10 9 8 7 6 5 4 3 2 1

To my in-laws:
Julie, Pete, Serena, Kristen

CONTENTS

Chapter One
GUMDROPS AND
TREASURE MAPS

I am Detective Dan.

I like to solve mysteries.

Mysteries are not hard to find.

Usually they find me!

One day I was reading my Bible.

I looked at my verse for the week.

And do not forget to do good and to share with others, for with such sacrifices God is pleased.
Hebrews 13:16

The verse made me think.

I needed to share more.

But what could I share?

Just then I heard a knock.

I opened my window.

Bernard was there.

"I need your help to find
some hidden treasure," he said.

I grabbed my detective coat.

I climbed out the window.

"What is the treasure?" I asked.

"It's a secret," answered Bernard.

"Whose treasure is it?" I asked him.

"Mine," Bernard said.

"I buried it in the ground last week.

Then I drew a treasure map

so I could find it again.

But I lost the map."

Bernard pulled his pocket
inside out.

"The map was in here," he said.

"It was a small map."

"What's in your other pocket?"
I asked.

"Gumdrops," Bernard said.

10

My mouth watered.
But I did not have time
to think about food.
I had a case to solve.
"When did you last see the map?"
I asked.
"This morning,"
said Bernard.
"I put it
in my pocket.
But it must
have fallen out."
"Then to find it,"
I said,
"we must go
everywhere
you went today."

"I will show you where I went,"
said Bernard.

He started walking.

I followed.

Newton, my dog, followed me.

We soon saw Mandy.

In her hand was a piece of paper.

"What are you holding?" I asked.

"Something special,"
answered Mandy.

"Is it a treasure map?"

asked Bernard.

"Yes," said Mandy.

I looked at the piece of paper.

It said:

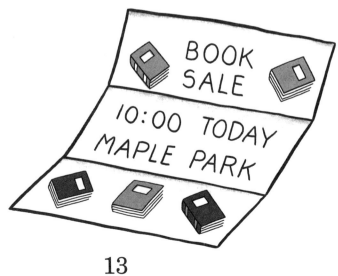

BOOK SALE

10:00 TODAY MAPLE PARK

"That isn't a treasure map," I said.

"It is to me," said Mandy.

"I treasure books. And this tells me where I can find some on sale."

She ran toward the park.

I thought about

what Mandy had said.

To her, books were a treasure.

I wondered what

Bernard's treasure was.

I would have to find

his missing map to find out.

Chapter Two
GUMDROP FUN

Bernard pulled a paper bag
from his pocket.
Two gumdrops fell to the ground.
Newton ate them.
Bernard ate some gumdrops too.

My stomach growled.

I looked at Bernard.

He looked at me.

"Oops," said Bernard.

"I almost forgot.

We have to find my treasure map."

He stuffed the bag back
into his pocket.

A piece of
the bag ripped.

The wind blew it
across the grass.

That gave me
an idea.

"Come on," I said.

"Let's follow that piece of the bag."

"Why?" asked Bernard.

"Your map might have
blown away," I said.

"And that piece of the bag
might lead us to the treasure map."

We followed the piece of paper bag.

It blew into the woods.

It stuck on a tree branch.

Under the tree was a pile of boards.

Sitting on the boards was Farley.

He did not look happy.

In his hand was a piece of paper.

In his pocket was a slingshot.

I had to be careful.

Newton agreed.

Farley stood up.

He crossed his arms.

"What are you doing here?"

he asked.

"Looking for something," I replied.

"Is that a map in your hand?"

"Come see," said Farley.

I stepped closer.

I looked at the piece of paper.

It was a plan for a tree house.

"I am building this," said Farley.

"And I will
have lots of
fun doing it.
Do you want
to have fun
with me?"
He smiled at me.

I looked at the plans again.

I looked at the pile of wood.

It looked like a lot of work.

"I am busy with a case," I said.

"How about you?"

Farley asked Bernard.

Bernard was eating gumdrops.

22

Newton was eating
the ones Bernard dropped.
"I am going to have lots of fun,"
said Farley.
"If you give me some gumdrops,
I will let
you have fun
with me."
Bernard
stuffed the
gumdrop bag
into his pocket.
"Sorry,"
Bernard said.
"I have only
enough gumdrops
for me."

Farley stopped smiling.

He looked angry.

Newton ran.

"We've got to go," I said.

"There's something very important
we have to do."

Bernard and I walked quickly away.

"What's the important thing
we have to do?" asked Bernard.

"Stay out of trouble," I said.

"We also have to solve this case,"
said Bernard.

He was right.

I just hoped solving the case
would not get us both into trouble.

Chapter Three
THE GUMDROP TRADE

"Show me where else
you went today," I said.
"First I need to rest," said Bernard.
He sat down on a rock.
He pulled out his bag of gumdrops.
Several dropped to the ground.

Newton ate them.

Bernard threw some gumdrops
into his mouth.

I sat next to him.

I looked at his bag.

I hoped he would share
some gumdrops with me.

But he did not.

I thought
about my verse
for the week.
And do not
forget to do good
and to share
with others, for with such sacrifices
God is pleased.
Bernard needed to share.
So did I.
I needed to share
my verse with him.

"Look!" said Bernard. Jasper, Tara's little brother, was running toward us.

In his hand was a piece of paper.

"He must have something
important," said Bernard.

"Tara is chasing him.

Maybe he has my map."

"Catch him!" yelled Tara.

I leaped for Jasper.

I pulled him to the ground.

The piece of paper flew into the air.

Scratch, Tara's cat, caught it
in her mouth.

"What is on the paper?" I asked.

"Something very special," said Tara.

She stepped toward Scratch.

Scratch showed her claws.

Tara stepped back.

So did I.

Newton hid behind my legs.

"What do we do now?" asked Tara.

"We have to get Scratch
to open her mouth," I said.

"How?" Tara asked.

"By giving her food," I answered.

"Look, Scratch. Yum!"
said Bernard.
He threw a gumdrop
toward Scratch.
Scratch looked at it.
But she did not eat it.
Then, slowly, Scratch yawned.
The piece of paper
dropped from her mouth.

TARA

Tara grabbed it.
"That's just
a drawing,"
I said.
"It's not
something special."

"Yes it is," said Tara.
"It's a drawing of me.
And I am very special."
She smiled and held up the picture.
I, Detective Dan,
did not want
to see it.
I wanted to see
a treasure map.
I wanted to solve
the case.

Chapter Four
GOOEY GUMDROPS

I started to walk away.

Something squished under my shoe.

It was the gumdrop

Bernard had thrown to Scratch.

Now it was a gooey gumdrop.

I tried to
wipe it off,
but it stuck like glue.
What a mess!
I looked at Bernard.
He was eating gumdrops again.
Newton was eating the ones
Bernard dropped.
I wanted to eat some gumdrops too.
But Bernard was still not sharing.

I walked up
to Bernard.
Grass stuck to
the squished
gumdrop
on my shoe.
"That's it!"
I said.
"That's what?"
asked Bernard.

"That's the clue I need to solve
this case," I told him.
"I don't understand," Bernard said.
"You like gumdrops," I said.
"And you like to keep them
all for yourself."
"What does that have to do

with finding my treasure map?"
asked Bernard.

"You keep dropping gumdrops,"
I said.

"And Newton keeps eating them.
But this morning, there was no one
to eat them. So where did they go?"

Bernard shrugged his shoulders.
"Maybe some animals ate
the dropped gumdrops," he said.
"Or maybe you kept them,"
I said, "just like I kept this one—
squished on the bottom
of your shoe."
Bernard picked up one of his feet.

On the bottom of his shoe was a
squished, gooey gumdrop.
Stuck to the gumdrop
was a small piece of paper.
"It's my map!" said Bernard.
"Your map dropped out of your
pocket this morning," I said.
"And it stuck to
the gumdrop on your shoe."

"Thanks for finding my map,"
said Bernard.

"What can I do to repay you?"

"Will you share some gumdrops
with me?" I asked.

Bernard held up an empty bag.

My stomach growled.

"Come with me," said Bernard.

He got a shovel.

He followed his treasure map.

Newton and I followed him.

"Here's the spot," said Bernard.

He dug into the ground.

He lifted out a box.

He opened the lid.

We looked inside.

It was a gooey mess.

"My gumdrops!" yelled Bernard.

"What happened? I can't eat these!"

"No one can eat them," I agreed.

"They are no good now.

Maybe you should not have hid

them for yourself.

Maybe you should have

shared them."

I shared my verse for the week
with Bernard.
Bernard looked at me.
He pulled a gumdrop
from his pocket.
"This one slipped out of the bag,"
he said.
"I was saving it to eat later.
But I want you to have it."
I took the gumdrop.
I smiled.

It had been a good day.

The case was solved.

The treasure was found.

Bernard was learning to share.

And I, Detective Dan, could finally
eat a gumdrop.
Which is what I did.

THE GOOEY GUMDROP
WRAP-UP REPORT

VERSE FOR THE WEEK:

"And do not forget to do good and to share

with others,

for with such sacrifices God is pleased."

Hebrews 13:16

THE CULPRIT: SELFISHNESS

Selfishness is keeping everything for yourself

instead of giving some of what you have

to others.

QUESTIONS TO EXPLORE AND ANSWER:

✔ Was Bernard selfish?

✔ Why didn't he share?

✔ What happened to his treasure?

✔ What does the Bible say about sharing?

✔ Do you like to share?

✔ Are there things that are hard for you to share?

✔ Why is sharing sometimes hard?

CONCLUSIONS:

✔ God doesn't want us to be selfish.

✔ Being selfish can hurt us.

It can also make us hurt others.

✔ Learn to share!

CASE CLOSED

Detective Dan

Did you enjoy this book about Detective Dan? I have good news—there are *more* Detective Dan books!

DETECTIVE DAN AND THE MISSING MARBLE MYSTERY
0-310-38091-X

DETECTIVE DAN AND THE PUZZLING PIZZA MYSTERY
0-310-38101-0

DETECTIVE DAN AND THE GOOEY GUMDROP MYSTERY
0-310-38111-8

DETECTIVE DAN AND THE FLYING FROG MYSTERY
0-310-38121-5

The Detective Dan books are available at your local Christian bookstore, or you can order direct from 800-727-3480.